# THE AMAZING FANTASTIC ROLLER SKATES

Story by Unice Y. Hsu

Illustrations by John Mansfield

The Amazing Fantastic Roller Skates

Copyright © 2010 by Unice Y. Hsu

All rights reserved. No part of this book may be reproduced or transmitted in any form or by any means without written permission of the author.

ISBN 978-201100143-600143

Paul was bored. He looked around his new room and could not find anything in there that he wanted to play with.

Paul left his room and started exploring his new house.

It was the beginning of summer. Paul, his little brother Joey, his little sister Jean, and their parents, Mr. and Mrs. Bell, had just moved into a new blue and white house in a new neighborhood a few days ago.

Paul's new house had a big front yard with a nice fence around it.

There was also another building next to his new house. Paul's father told Paul it was called a garage and it was a house for their car. Paul had explored the garage earlier and besides their car, there were only some old scrap pieces of wood and some rusty looking old tools.

Paul continued to explore the upstairs of his new house. When he was done, Paul went downstairs to the kitchen where his mother, Mrs. Bell was busy unpacking.

Paul said to his mother, "Mom, I'm bored."

Paul's mom suggested he go read a book. Paul shook his head no. Paul's mom suggested he go play with his little brother Joey. Paul shook his head no. Paul's little sister Jean was just a baby so

Paul's mom did not suggest that Paul go play with her.

Paul's mom suggested he go outside and maybe he could make some new friends.

Paul went outside. He saw some kids playing ball down the street.

Paul was shy and did not go join them.

Paul walked over to the garage where his father, Mr. Bell was working on their car.

Paul said to his dad, "Dad, I'm bored."

Paul's dad suggested he go inside and read a book. Paul shook his head no.

Paul's dad suggested he go inside and play with his little brother Joey. Paul shook his head no. Paul's dad also did not suggest he go inside and play with his baby sister Jean. Paul's dad suggested he go down the street and play ball with the other kids in the neighborhood. Paul went back inside his new house.

He went up the stairs two at a time and kept going until he stopped at the attic stairs.

Paul had not explored the attic yet, so he decided it would be a good idea. He climbed the stairs to the attic and turned on the lights.

He started looking through some boxes that his father had stored in there when they first moved to Paul's new house. He found one box which turned out to be full of old toys.

Inside the box he found some old rubber bouncy balls, a not so fluffy any more half stuffed teddy bear, a deflated kick-ball, an old baseball bat, and a pair of metal somethings which had wheels on the bottom.

Paul grabbed those metal somethings and took them downstairs to show his mother.

"Mom, what are these?" Paul asked, holding up the pair of metal somethings.

Paul's mom told him those were roller skates. She said they probably belonged to his father and he should go ask his father about them.

Paul went back outside and in the garage with the roller skates.

"Dad, Mom said these roller skates might be yours. Are they? Why do they look so strange? Can you show me how they work?" Inquired a very curious Paul.

Paul's dad said they were his old roller skates and he had played with them when he was Paul's age. Paul's dad also said they came with a key which was used to fit the roller skates to his feet.

Paul's dad went into the house and up into the attic. He returned back outside with a metal key.

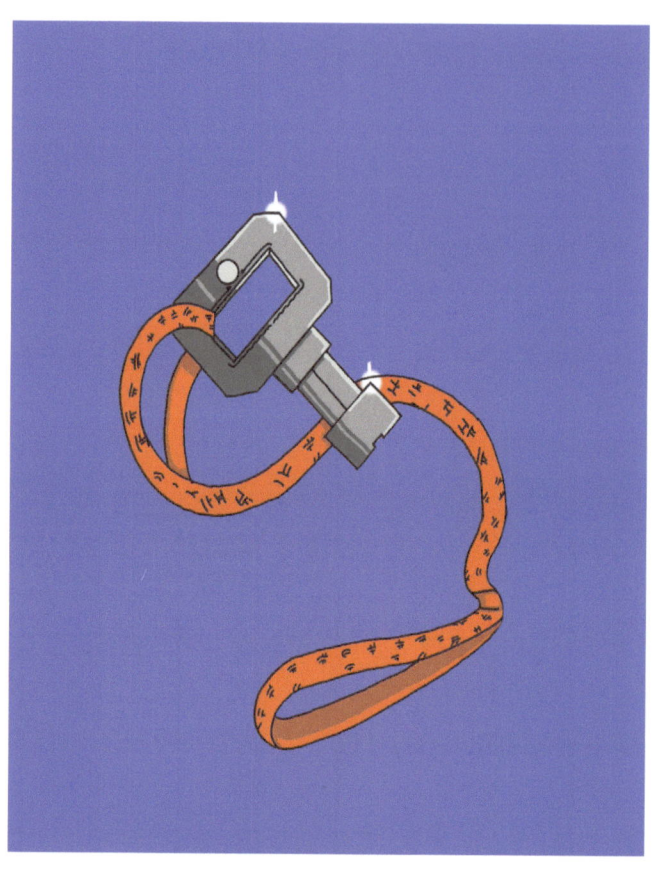

Paul's dad fit the key into the keyhole on the bottom of the roller skates and adjusted them to fit on Paul's shoes.

Paul was not bored anymore. He was happy. He started roller skating outside. He was having fun.

After a while, the neighborhood kids came to Paul's house. They saw him roller skating around in front of his house.

They gathered around Paul and introduced themselves.

"My name is Paul," Paul told the neighborhood kids. The kids kept looking down at Paul, curious to see what those metal somethings were on Paul's feet.

"They're roller skates," said Paul.

The neighborhood kids laughed. They said Paul's roller skates were just old junk and they looked goofy. They said that real roller skates didn't have wheels like Paul's and they weren't made of metal either. The neighborhood kids laughed as they left to go back to play ball down the street. Paul roller skated around some more but he wasn't having as much fun as he had earlier. Paul went back inside his new house.

The next day, Paul got his roller skates and went into his garage. He was in there for quite a while.

When Paul came out of his garage, he was holding a piece of wood that had wheels on the bottom.

Paul had taken the wheels off of his Dad's roller skates and attached them to an old piece of board he had found in the garage. Paul had turned his Dad's old roller skates into a skate board.

Paul started skate boarding on his skate board. Paul was happy. Paul was having fun.

Soon, the neighborhood kids came out to play. They stopped in front of Paul's house where Paul was skate boarding. They gathered around Paul, once again curious to see what Paul was playing with.

"It's a skate board," said Paul.

Again, the neighborhood kids laughed. They said Paul's skate board looked too homemade and would probably fall apart. They said Paul probably wouldn't even be able to do any tricks with it.  The neighborhood kids laughed and left to go play ball down the street.

Paul skate boarded by himself for a little while longer, but he wasn't as happy as he was earlier.  Skate boarding wasn't as much fun any more.  Paul went back inside his new house.

The next morning, Paul went back inside his garage with his skate board.  Paul had found some other pieces of scrap wood and built onto his skate board.  A few hours later, Paul came out pushing a scooter.

Paul happily scooted himself around his neighborhood. He was having so much fun!

Like the day before, the neighborhood kids came out to play. They stopped in front of Paul's house and once again, they gathered around him.

"I built a scooter," said Paul.

The neighborhood kids started laughing again. They said that Paul's scooter looked more rickety than his skate board. They continued laughing as they ran off down the street to play ball. Paul scooted around for a little while longer, but he did not find it fun any more. Paul went back inside his new house.

The following morning, Paul went into his garage with his scooter. He stayed in his garage most of the morning.

When he came out, Paul was pushing a go-kart! Paul had added more wood to his scooter and built a go-kart.

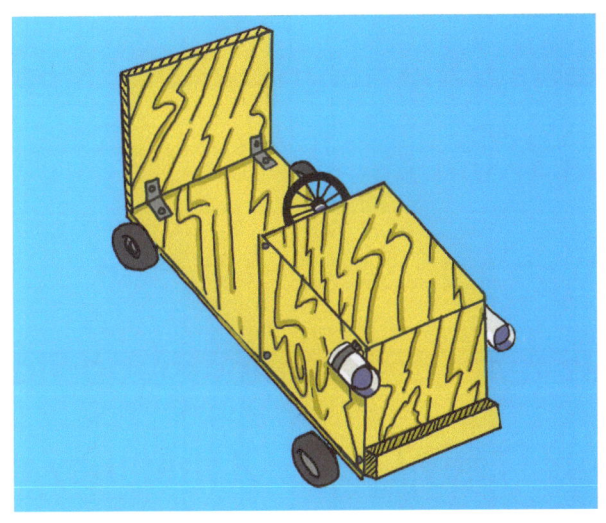

Paul would take his go-kart to the top of his driveway and push it a little and jump in and ride to the bottom. Paul did this for a while and he was having so much fun! The neighborhood kids heard the sound of Paul's go-kart and came over to Paul's house to see what was making the sound.

As Paul came to a stop at the end of his driveway, the neighborhood kids gathered around him.

"I built a go-kart," said Paul.

This time, the neighborhood kids did not laugh. They told Paul that they thought the go-kart was so cool.

They all wanted to ride in Paul's go-kart. Paul let them.

One by one, each of the neighborhood kids got a chance to ride in the go-kart. They played together until it got dark and everybody had to return home.

The next morning Paul pushed his go-kart into the garage. Paul also had a box of things under his arm.

When Paul came out of the garage, he was pushing his go-kart but it looked a little different. Paul had found an old bicycle horn and had attached it to his go-kart. He also found a bicycle headlamp which was now attached to the front of his go-kart. He also built a seat using some old wood and an old pillow he found in the attic.

Paul played with his new and improved go-kart. The neighborhood kids came over to Paul's driveway.

"This is my amazing go-kart," said Paul. "It now has a horn, a light, and a nice soft seat."

They all took turns in Paul's go-kart and played until it got dark. All the kids went home including Paul.

The next day, Paul pushed his amazing go-kart into the garage again. And like the day before, he had a box with him. This time, the box was bigger and Paul put it in his amazing go-kart since he couldn't carry it.

When Paul came out of his garage, he was pushing a newly painted red go-kart with wood plank doors and a new foot controlled steering system (also made of wood). Paul tested out his new wood steering system and found out that it worked just fine.

The neighborhood kids came to Paul's driveway.

Paul said to them, "This is my amazing red go-kart." The neighborhood kids told Paul it was even cooler than before. They took turns on the go-kart and played until it got dark and they all went home.

The next day, Paul pushed his amazing red go-kart back into the garage. A little while later, Paul pushed his go-kart out of the garage and to the driveway. Paul's go-kart now had the word "AMAZING" painted in black on one door, the word "FANTASTIC" on the other, and the words "go-kart" painted on the back of the go-kart seat. Paul's amazing red go-kart now also had special wooden hand brakes which could slow the amazing red go-kart down.

Paul went to the top of his driveway and tested the new wooden hand brakes of his amazing red go-kart. He was having so much fun. The neighborhood kids gathered around Paul and his go-kart.

"My AMAZING FANTASTIC red go-kart has brakes now," Paul announced to the neighborhood kids.

The neighborhood kids told Paul that his AMAZING FANTASTIC red go-kart was absolutely the coolest AMAZING FANTASTIC red go-kart they had ever seen!

**They**

all

**took**

turns

on Paul's coolest AMAZING FANTASTIC red go-kart until it got dark and everyone had to return home.

The next morning Paul did not go into his garage. He came out of his house and pushed his AMAZING FANTASTIC red go-kart to the top of his driveway and go-karted all morning.

When the neighborhood kids came to Paul's driveway, they all took turns and played until dark. They had so much fun.

They played with Paul and his AMAZING FANTASTIC red go-kart for days and days.

One morning, while Paul and the neighborhood kids were out playing with Paul's AMAZING FANTASTIC red go-kart, there was a crash!

Paul was riding down the driveway and tried to pull up on the hand brake. When Paul pulled up on the brake, his hand slipped off of one side of the steering plank and the **AMAZING FANTASTIC** red go-kart curved too hard and crashed into the big oak tree at the side of Paul's driveway!

Paul went soaring out of the AMAZING FANTASTIC red go-kart and landed on the sidewalk a few feet away. Paul's AMAZING FANTASTIC red go-kart was smashed to pieces. The neighborhood kids ran to Paul to see if he was hurt. Paul was not hurt. They all gathered at the big oak tree and looked around at the pieces of what was Paul's AMAZING FANTASTIC red go-kart.

The pieces of the go-kart did not look so AMAZING or FANTASTIC anymore. One of the neighborhood kids suggested that they go down the street to play ball. The neighborhood kids all left. Paul picked up the pieces of what was his AMAZING

FANTASTIC red go-kart and put the pieces in his garage. Paul went inside his house.

The next morning, Paul went inside his garage. When he came out later, he had on his dad's old roller skates. Paul started roller skating in front of his house. After a while, the neighborhood kids came to Paul's house. They gathered around Paul.

"These roller skates are so much fun. They're really AMAZING and FANTASTIC, too!" said Paul.

The neighborhood kids all agreed with Paul. They all took turns with Paul's AMAZING FANTASTIC roller skates. They played until it got dark outside and they all had to return home.

For the rest of the summer, Paul and his friends had fun playing together.

**THE END**

www.ingramcontent.com/pod-product-compliance
Ingram Content Group UK Ltd.
Pitfield, Milton Keynes, MK11 3LW, UK
UKHW060453210426
11947UKWH00047B/3